P9-CKY-076

Vera B Williams
A CHAIR FOR ALWAYS

Greenwillow Books, *An Imprint of* HarperCollins*Publishers*

A Chair for Always. Copyright © 2009 by Vera B. Williams. All rights reserved.
Printed in the United States of America.
www.harpercollinschildrens.com
All rights reserved. No part of this book may be used or reproduced in any manner whatsoever without written permission
except in the case of brief quotations embodied in critical articles and reviews. For information address
HarperCollins Children's Books, a division of HarperCollins Publishers, 1350 Avenue of the Americas, New York, NY 10019.

Gouache was used to prepare the full-color art. The text type is Zapf Book.

Library of Congress Cataloging-in-Publication Data

Williams, Vera B. A chair for always / by Vera B. Williams.
p. cm. "Greenwillow Books."
Summary: Rosa is excited when her new cousin, Benji, is born, but when Grandma wants to remove a beloved armchair,
Rosa puts her foot down and insists that the chair, just like Benji, is a member of the family.
ISBN 978-0-06-172279-0 (trade bdg.)—ISBN 978-0-06-172280-6 (lib. bdg.)
ISBN 978-0-06-172283-7 (Spanish trade bdg.)—ISBN 978-0-06-172643-9 (Spanish pbk.)
[1. Chairs—Fiction. 2. Babies—Fiction. 3. Family life—Fiction.] I. Title.
PZ7.W6685Cf 2009   [E]—dc22   2008027719

09 10 11 12 13 CG/WORZ First Edition 10 9 8 7 6 5 4 3 2 1

 Greenwillow Books

Rosa's Mom at the Blue Tile Diner

My mother worked so late at the Blue Tile Diner that Grandma and I fell asleep in our big chair waiting for her. Grandma woke a little around midnight.

"Pussycat," she said, "look at us asleep in this chair like two mice in a nest. Go get in bed. Kids like you need to dream."

Grandma tucked me in, same as she does every night.

Right after I settle my head down into my pillow she whispers, "Wait a minute," and pulls the pillow out from under my head. She plumps it up and holds it by her cheek. Then she tucks it back under my head. "There, now you'll dream good!" she says.

"Leave the door open a little," I always tell her. I get scared if I can't see down the hall to Mama's room.

Then I fell asleep. But I woke up so suddenly early in the morning, before it was light.

What a strange quiet, with everyone on our block asleep. I tiptoed down the hall to peek into my mother's room. There were her waitress shoes, right where she stepped out of them. And there she was, flopped on her side with the bedspread pulled up over her shoulder like always when she comes home late. So everything was all right, and I was going to sneak in next to her and go back to sleep.

But I heard a door scrape open upstairs, where Uncle Sandy and Aunt Ida live . . . then footsteps and Aunt Ida's voice. It woke my mother right up. Grandma's light went on. Then the phone rang and I heard Grandma say, "I'll be up in a minute."

Mama came rushing and bumped right into me. "It's only four in the morning," she said, and pushed me into her room. "There, sleep in my bed. It's all warm already."

"But where are you going?" I asked her. "What's wrong?"

"Wrong!" She laughed.

"Aunt Ida's baby is starting to get born."

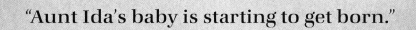

I jumped up. "I'll come too," I called after her.

"No way! You stay right here. Wish really hard for an easy birth for the baby and your auntie."

"But I want to help too," I said. "That's my cousin in Aunt Ida's belly." My mother hesitated a second.

"Please!" I begged.

"You're too young," she told me. "But I promise I'll come get you the minute the baby is born! And I need you to do an important job. When the alarm rings, call Josephine at the diner. Tell her I'll have to be late. Explain how the baby is being born at home, so I need to help my sister."

I slept and I didn't sleep. I held my teddy bear. He's slept with me since our house burned down. That's when we moved in here with Aunt Ida and Uncle Sandy upstairs.

Aunt Ida is a singer. She helps us with our band: the Oak Street Band.

I reminded Teddy Bear how Aunt Ida was always saying we needed a guitar in our band, and joking how she would give birth to a baby who would be born knowing how to play the guitar.

Then there could be five of us: me on the accordion, Leora on the drums, Jenny on the violin, Mae with the flute, and Baby on the guitar.

I heard someone ring the front doorbell. I knew it was the midwife, come to help the baby get safely born.

There had been many arguments at our house about whether it was better for the baby to be born at home or at the hospital like lots of babies. But Aunt Ida wanted the baby born in the midst of her family, in her own house. She said she would go to the hospital for sure if there was some kind of emergency, and you can believe Uncle Sandy had the car ready just in case.

I dozed off wondering whether maybe it was twins. Aunt Ida's belly was so so big! But my mother had explained to me how when I got born her belly looked as big with just tiny me, who had weighed in at six pounds, one ounce.

I was startled when the alarm went off. Then I remembered and called up my mother's boss, Josephine, to give her the message.

"Oh honey, wish your aunt good luck from me," she said. "And Rosa, don't be impatient. It can take a long time to get born."

"How long?" I asked her.

"Well," she said, "my first baby took twenty-four hours. But the second took only four. He came fast."

"I could never wait even four hours," I told Josephine.

Josephine knows me. Sometimes I help out at the diner and Josephine pays me. That was part of the money we saved up in the jar to get the wonderful armchair for my mother, after the fire had burned up all our furniture. And there was that same chair, still right there in our living room.

I decided that it was very important for me to get out of my ma's bed and to wait right in our chair.

Our chair is a lucky chair.

I would sit in the chair and imagine.
I am a very good imaginer.

Now, I imagined a tiny baby that would look a lot like me, though the Well Baby Clinic already informed Aunt Ida and Uncle Sandy that their baby is a boy. I do love Uncle Sandy, so they should name the baby Benjamin, which is Uncle Sandy's real name. A boy would keep Uncle Sandy company. Sometimes when we're all having dinner together, Uncle Sandy looks around and says, "Females . . . as far as the eye can see."

A boy. Yes, a tiny boy. I imagined him with his tiny guitar. I could see it already, hidden right in his ear when he was born, which made me laugh.

I imagined filling up our money jar again. Someday we could buy him a bigger guitar and a keyboard for me.

I imagined teaching him to read, taking him to the library, getting him a tiny strawberry ice cream cone. I imagined arguing with him and telling him that *I was right* because *I was older*. I imagined and imagined . . . myself right to sleep.

"Rosa, wake up," my mom said.

And she pulled and pushed sleepy me up the stairs to meet my brand-new cousin.

And there he was.

Aunt Ida looked so happy. Uncle Sandy looked so happy.

Mama looked happy,

and my grandma looked super happy.

Our midwife looked happy too.

So did the bed, the chairs, the table,

the window, the loaf of bread on the table,

the cups and saucers. And me, of course.

Of course . . . ME, Cousin Rosa, who was so lucky

to be right there when a completely new human

had just been born.

I ran up and down the stairs all those next days, visiting the baby and helping Aunt Ida.

She showed me how to hold him so his head didn't bobble. I helped Uncle Sandy bathe him. Those eight pounds, four ounces of him were very slippery.

I told him the story of how we got our chair. I could tell I was going to love telling him stories.

Then my friends Leora, Jenny, and Mae, from the Oak Street Band, came over to see him. Leora said we had to wash our hands, and then we squinched into the chair. Aunt Ida put the baby on my lap. Mae got out her flute and played him a lullaby.

It was beautiful, but my grandma was not content.

"You know," she said, "that chair is getting worn out. It used to be a chair for your mother. Now it's a chair for you and your friends and for little Benji. I think the chair should be all clean and new for my new grandbaby."

Grandma was just itching to reupholster that chair! Once, even before Benji was born, I saw her standing in front of our chair with big scissors and a lot of fabric lying all around!

"Oh no, you can't change our chair, Grandma. It's perfect just the way it's always been," I told her then. But now the seat gets damp from Baby Benji's wet diaper. The cushion is worn and faded.

So we just made a new cover for the seat and back cushions. Then Uncle Sandy and I took a bunch of photos.

Rosa Pretending to be Grandma

But Grandma went right on muttering, and I could tell that even my mother began to have secret thoughts.

One Sunday morning she said, "Rosa, what do you think? Maybe now with my pay raise we could save up enough money to buy a brand-new chair?" She was looking at the Sunday paper furniture sales.

But I *had* to tell her, just as I had told Grandma, "No. Absolutely and Positively No! This chair is going to last forever. And I don't care about stains. Then when I grow up and Benji grows up and you are maybe a grandma and Grandma turns into a great-grandma, then her great-grandbaby can sit right here in this same chair."

My mother was laughing. I had to give her one of my very serious looks.

"Don't you even care about history?" I asked her. "Don't you even remember how you brought home the jar, and how we saved all those quarters and dimes and nickels . . . even pennies! And how we started the band and how the money we made with the band went into the jar too?"

"Oh you," she said. "You! You always want everything to stay just like it is. But maybe someday we'll move. I'll surely get old. Grandma will get even older. Baby Benji will get big faster than you think. And you will grow up, and who knows what you'll do."

"Maybe you'll even become president and move away to the White House in Washington. Everything changes, you know."

"But not this chair," I said. I ran my hands over the beloved velvet roses on the arms. "NOT THIS CHAIR! And wherever I go, this chair goes too!"

Mama gave me one of her famous exasperated sighs.

"How come you think you know that?" she asked.

"Because," I said. "Because my name is Rosa, and there are things I just know."

This time my mother didn't sigh. She gave me one of her famous hugs. "Rosa," she said, "you sure do say the strangest things."

Then she whispered in my ear so close it tickled, "But I love you best of all."

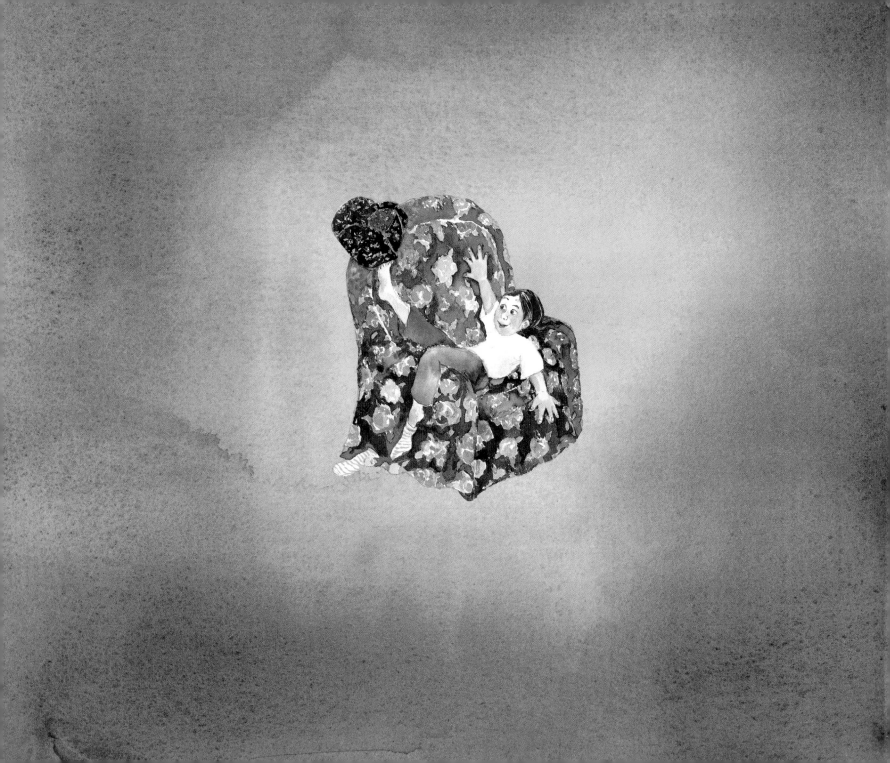